Rachel Field

GENERAL STORE

illustrated by
Nancy Winslow Parker

Greenwillow Books, New York

For Applegate's Hardware Store
Paints, Housewares, Sportswear, Toys
Founded 1895

Grateful acknowledgement is made to:
Wheaton Village Museum of American Glass, Gay L. Taylor, Curator
Point Pleasant Library, Barbara Kaden, Chief Librarian • The New York Historical Society
The New York Public Library • Joe Delengyel, Jersey Shore Bottle Club
Patricia Wojcik, Tax Collector and Treasurer, Borough of Bay Head
The Kellogg Company, for permission to reproduce the SALADA® trademark

Sarsaparilla oil, a flavoring agent, is made from the roots of the evergreen shrub, *smilax regelli*.
Sarsaparilla soda was a popular soft drink in the 1920s. Today, sarsaparilla is still used as a flavoring in root beer.

Watercolors, colored pencils, and a black pen were used for the full-color art.
The text type is ITC Garamond.

Text copyright © 1926 by Rachel Field
Illustrations copyright © 1988 by Nancy Winslow Parker

All rights reserved.

No part of this book may be reproduced or utilized in any form or by any means, electronic or mechanical, including photocopying, recording or by any information storage and retrieval system, without permission in writing from the Publisher, Greenwillow Books, a division of William Morrow & Company, Inc., 105 Madison Avenue, New York, N.Y. 10016.
Printed in Singapore by Tien Wah Press
First Edition   10 9 8 7 6 5 4 3 2 1

Library of Congress Cataloging-in-Publication Data
Field, Rachel, 1894-1942.   General store/by Rachel Field; pictures by Nancy Winslow Parker.
p.   cm.   Summary: A girl imagines the general store she will own some day and all the things for sale in it, from bolts of calico to bunches of bananas.
ISBN 0-688-07353-0. ISBN 0-688-07354-9 (lib. ed.)
[1. General stores—Fiction.   2. Stores, Retail—Fiction.
3. Stories in rhyme.]   I. Parker, Nancy Winslow, ill.
II. Title.   PZ8.3.F456Ge 1988   [E]—dc19
87-21641   CIP   AC

Someday I'm going to have—

a store!

With a tinkly bell hung over the door,

with real glass cases and counters wide,
and drawers all spilly with things inside.

There'll be a little of everything:
bolts of calico,

balls of string,

jars of peppermint,

tins of tea,

pots,

and kettles,

and crockery.

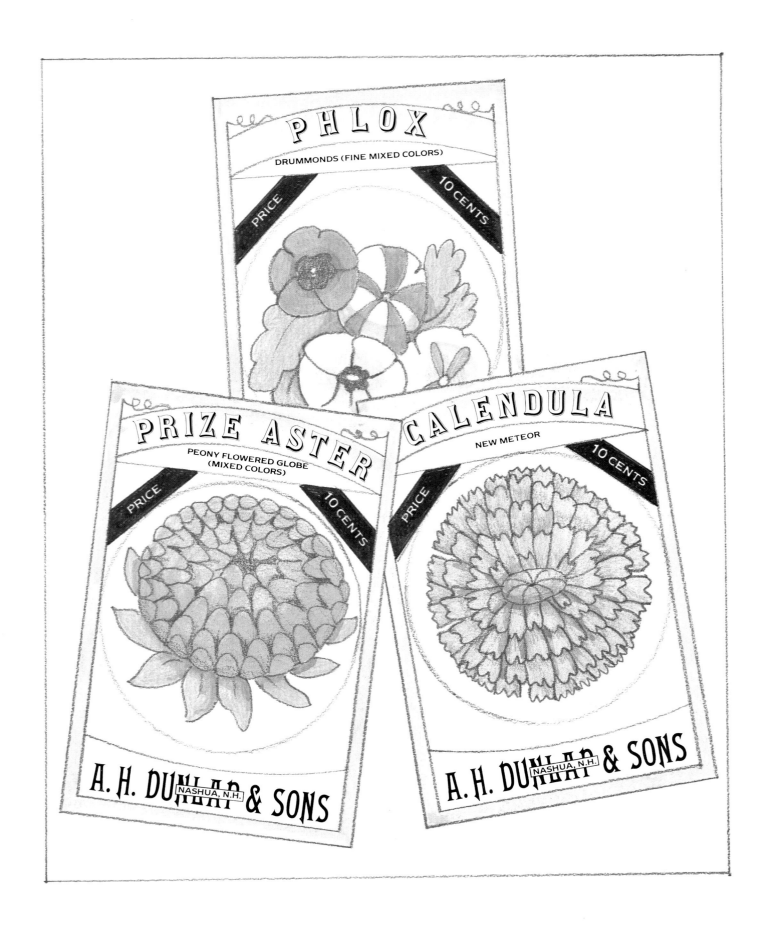

Seeds in packets,

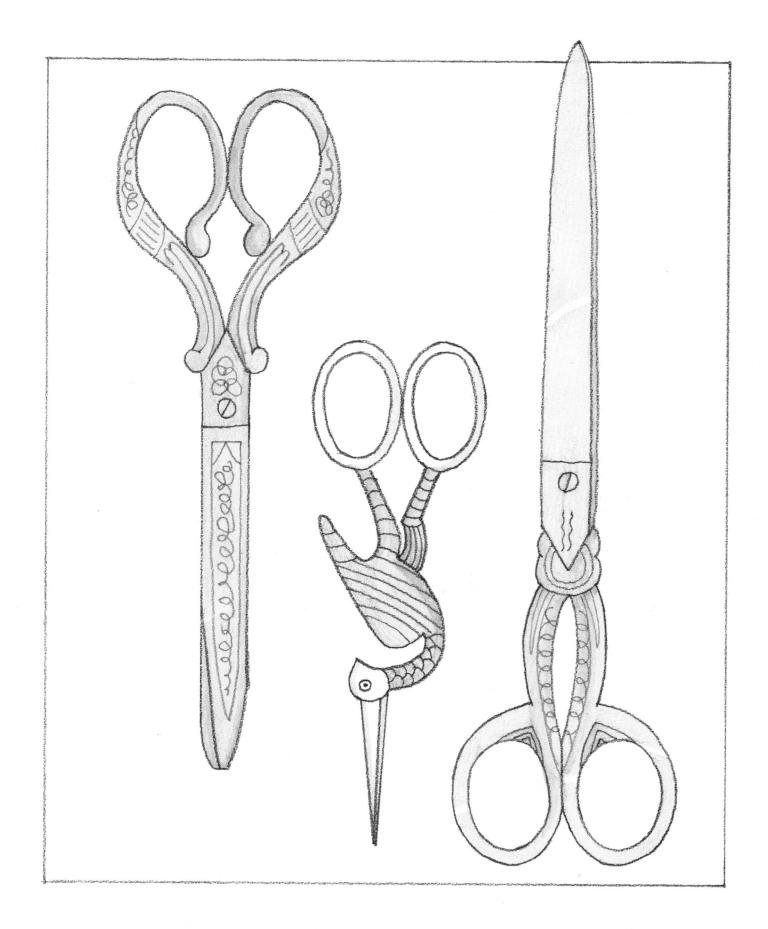

scissors bright,

kegs of sugar,

brown and white.

Sarsaparilla for picnic lunches,

bananas and rubber boots in bunches.

I'll fix the window

and dust each shelf,

and take the money in all myself.

It will be my store and I will say,

"What can I do for you today?"